Introduction

These stories were written in 1952 for Edith Cameron Wagner's first grandchild, Lorna Christine Meier, who had to spend weeks in bed while recovering from an illness.
Inspired by the squirrels playing in the big elm trees in her yard, the stories were begun. The names Scampy and Frisky came from two small ceramic squirrels that resided on a shelf in her living room. Grandma Edie, or Nana, as she was called, wrote a story each day to entertain her usually active seven-year-old grand-daughter.
Years later, after Lori married and had children of her own, she illustrated the stories as a tribute to her grandmother and what the stories had meant to her.
Now, with this printing, the antics of Scampy and Frisky and their friends can be enjoyed by more grandchildren and great-grandchildren.

Artist's Dedication

to

Edith Cameron Wagner

Grandmother (Nana), Writer

Who Shared Her Talent and Love

With Me with these

Stories

May They Now be Shared

With Many Others

Lori Meier Kay

Contents

BIG BROWN DOG WANTS TO PLAY

In a big oak tree in a small woodsy part of land lived two little Squirrels with their mother and father squirrel.

The woods were near a brown house in which lived a very nice family -- a mother, a father, and a little girl.

The squirrels were named Scampy and Frisky because they were never still, but were always running and jumping and playing games with each other.

They liked to watch the little girl play. One day the little girl fell off her bicycle, bumping her head and bruising her knee. Scampy and Frisky, who were playing tag in a walnut tree nearby, stopped their play to see what would happen, they felt so sorry for the little girl.

They were very happy when the mother came hurrying out of the house, wiped the tears away and wrapped up the injured knee; soon the little girl was smiling again.

One day a big brown dog who lived in the house was running all around the yard. He had been tied up for a long time, and was so happy to be loose he didn't know what to do. It was springtime, and he could smell all the spring fragrance in the air.

Suddenly he saw Scampy and Frisky, who were chasing each other up and down the tree trunks, and he thought..."That looks like fun—I wish I were a squirrel and could play with them—guess I'll go over and ask them if they'll play something I can play."

(Dogs of course couldn't run up and down tree trunks.)

So he ran swiftly over to them. The little squirrels saw him coming and were very frightened, because he was so very much bigger than they, and their mother had taught them that dogs would chase little squirrels.

As quick as a flash they ran up the tree which held their nest. They were trembling when they tumbled in beside their mother, who had been watching them anxiously. She chattered and scolded them for not seeing the big dog sooner.

They peeked over the top of the nest and could see him, sitting on the ground looking up into the tree, and wondering what had become of those funny little animals he wanted to play with.

He didn't know they were afraid of him, or he probably would have had his feelings hurt, and have cried "doggy tears".

The mother squirrel quieted Scampy and Frisky. They were so happy to be safe and sound.
As mother squirrel prepared walnuts for supper she said she hoped they would be more careful in the future.
That night Scampy and Frisky snuggled down to go to sleep thinking about new playmates and adventures with new friends.

LITTLE MOUSE HAS A BIG SCARE

One day Scampy and Frisky decided to go for a long walk. Their mother told them not to stay away too long because she was making a delicious nut pudding for their supper.

As they played hide and seek around the bushes and trees, they were wishing something exciting would happen. Just then the little girl, who was outside her playhouse, gave a funny little "EEK" and called "Mommy, mommy, come quickly, there's a little mouse."

Before Scampy and Frisky could move, the little mouse scampered past them so fast all they could see was his tail! He disappeared in the bushes.

Then very softly, Scampy and Frisky followed him and said "Hello, come on out and play – we didn't mean to scare you." The little mouse looked around the corner of a big green leaf and said "Who are you?"

The little squirrels told him they lived in the big oak tree. Very cautiously the little mouse came out of his hiding place and sat down in the grass. "My name is Squeaky – give me a minute to catch my breath," he said. I really had to run when that little girl screamed. Why did she do it? What was the matter with her? I was just watching her play."

Scampy scratched his ear thoughtfully. "Well, maybe she is just as afraid of you as you are of her - did you think of that?" "How could she be?" said the mouse. She's so much bigger than I am." "Yes, said Frisky "but you frightened her. She wasn't expecting to see you there. That was the reason. You know you and all your little cousins and uncles and aunts are known for stealing food. You also eat bits of food or things you find in people's houses."

"Not me "said the little mouse firmly, "not me. I wouldn't steal anything." But he decided from then on he'd stay away from the brown house and play in the woods with Scampy and Frisky.

BENNY BUNNY GETS LOST

One sunny day when mother squirrel told Scampy and Frisky they could go out to play, they scampered down the tree trunk. They played games until they were tired and then sat down to rest.

Suddenly they saw a rabbit hopping toward them--it was Jimmy Cottontail. He looked so worried and so troubled that they asked him what was the matter. He told them his little brother Benny Bunny was lost, and Mother Bunny had sent him out to look for Benny.

Scampy and Frisky offered to help him, and that made him very happy. So the little squirrels ran and the bunny hopped, and they looked and looked, but couldn't find little Benny anywhere.

Now it happened that Grandma Rabbit was going home to her little house in the woods; she had been to see Aunt Mary Rabbit, who was very sick. Grandma Rabbit had made her some very good carrot soup and she said it had made her feel better already.

Grandma Rabbit was hopping along when she thought she heard somebody crying. She listened and looked, but couldn't see anybody, so she hurried on. Then she heard the crying again, and stopped to look all around her very carefully.

There, under a big raspberry bush she saw a little rabbit crying so hard he didn't see her. She hopped up to him and said: "What is the matter? My goodness, you're making so much noise you'll frighten all the little birds right out of their nests. Tell me what's the trouble? "

Grandma Rabbit wasn't Benny's real grandma, but she was such a nice little old lady rabbit that everybody loved her and called her grandma. So, she didn't know Benny's name, or where he lived.

Benny told her he had gone too far from home trying to see where a beautiful blue and gold butterfly was going, and now he couldn't find his way back.

Grandma decided someone would soon come to find him, so she told him she'd stay with him until they came. While they waited she told him stories all about the lovely flowers and beautiful butterflies and all the fun she had when she was a little girl bunny.

Benny loved listening to the stories so much that he forgot he was lost.

Meanwhile Scampy, Frisky and Jimmy Cottontail were still looking for little lost Benny. Suddenly they heard Grandma Bunny's voice, and could hear her and Benny talking.

They ran and hopped as fast as they could and soon saw them. How happy they were to find Benny!

Grandma Rabbit told them to come soon to visit her and she'd have a tea party for them -- with carrot cakes for the bunnies, and nut cakes for the little squirrels. They thanked her so much for staying with little Benny, and for her kind invitation.

On the way home little Benny Bunny promised he'd never hop so far away again.

BUSY ANT TEACHES SCAMPY AND FRISKY A LESSON

Frisky came running out to play but couldn't see Scampy anywhere. Finally, he saw him sitting very quietly watching something on the sidewalk.

"What are you doing" he called, "What's the matter, can't you move or are you playing "statues" all by yourself?"

"Shsh" said Scampy, "be quiet. I'm watching this busy little ant. I can't figure out what it's doing." Frisky sat down beside him to see if he could tell what interested his little brother so much.
The little ant carrying a big crumb bigger than it was, worked and tugged and pulled until it had the load across the sidewalk where it disappeared into the grass.
In a minute it was back and then hurried away, paying no attention to anyone or anything. As they watched intently, it came back again, they couldn't tell from where, with another huge bread crumb. This time it couldn't move the big load. The ant hurried back to where it had obtained the big crumb and soon another ant came out. Together they pushed and pulled and lifted their load until they had it across the walk and into the grass, where they disappeared from sight.

"My goodness", said Scampy, it makes me tired just to watch them, they have to work so hard." "Me too", said Frisky. "I'm all worn out and I haven't done a thing but look."

The next trip the little ant made, Frisky said to him "Excuse us Mr. Ant, but will you tell us what you're doing?"

"Don't bother me - don't bother me," he said crossly," I'll never get finished. I have too much to do before winter comes." "Winter," said Frisky." That's a long way off - why worry about the winter now."

"We have to see that our storehouses underground are full of food for the cold weather," replied the busy little ant, "and we have to do it now while the days are nice and we can find the food. You're too young to know, but squirrels store nuts for the winter too. When you're older you'll also have to help. Goodbye now, I have to get back to work."

"Oh dear", said Scampy, "let's play and have fun while we're young. Pretty soon we will have to work hard storing nuts for the winter."

They ran off to play but didn't forget about the busy little ants or the lesson they learned.

SINGING LESSONS

Scampy and Frisky heard sweet singing one day coming from the branches of an old oak tree. They came nearer and saw a sign which read - "Miss Jenny Wren -Teacher of Singing" - they stopped in surprise they'd never heard of anything like that before.

Miss Jenny Wren flew down beside them from her perch in front of the little birds who were in her singing class. She wore a little yellow bonnet and shawl because it was a coo l, spring day. She said cheerfully, "Hello, little squirrels, did you want to join my class and learn to sing?" Jenny Wren laughed merrily because who ever heard of a little squirrel singing!

"Oh no, Miss Jenny Wren", they said but we'd like to listen if you don't mind." She told them they could stay until after the class was over and then they were going to have a tea party.

So Scampy and Frisky listened attentively while all the little birds in the class sang and sang their sweet songs.

"I wish I could sing like that," said Scampy wistfully. "If you were supposed to sing, you would be able to" said Frisky sensibly - you're supposed to be a little squirrel so why not be happy about it.

Anyway, little birds can't run up and down the trees like you can or gather nuts." Scampy decided Frisky was right and he wouldn't feel badly because he didn't have a sweet voice.

After the singing lesson was over, Scampy and Frisky enjoyed the tea party with all the little birds. After that day, they came often to listen to Miss Jenny Wren's singing class.

SCAMPY AND FRISKY HEAR A MYSTERIOUS NOISE

"This is a fine day for a picnic", said Scampy one warm spring day. "Let's ask mother squirrel to make us some sandwiches and we'll go down by the brook."

Mother squirrel was busy house cleaning - she had a gingham apron on, and was working so hard she didn't hear Scampy at first. But then, she smiled and said she'd fix their lunch right away. She made some nice little nut sandwiches and gave them each a big nice carrot and off they ran.

Scampy and Frisky had a wonderful time – all along the way they met their little friends and stopped to talk to them and pretty soon they came to the brook. It was so quiet they could hear the water rippling over the smooth white stones and the bees buzzing as they flew over the flowers growing by the side of the stream.

They ate their lunch and had a refreshing drink of nice, cold water. "Let's take a nap before we start back home" said Frisky. "It's so warm and I'm so sleepy."

Just then they heard a big noise. It sounded like "Grrrmp-Grrmp" - and was so loud they both jumped up in the air. "What was that?" said Frisky. "I don't know," said Scampy. They both sat very still, too frightened to move.

"Ho, ho," said a big hearty voice. When the little squirrels looked out on the water, there was a fat old frog sitting on a big leaf. He was laughing so hard he shook and all of a sudden splash! He fell into the water.

Almost immediately he was out again and said "It's a good thing I know how to swim, little squirrels, isn't it? What're your names? I hope I didn't frighten you when I laughed so hard."

They told him their names and he said everyone called him "Grandpa Frog" because he was so old, nobody knew how old he was.

He told them interesting stories of the things he'd seen all the years he'd lived in the brook. Before they knew it, it was time to go home. Grandpa Frog told them to be sure to come back and he'd tell them some more stories.

Grandpa Frogs fall into the brook would be a story Scampy and Frisky would share with their mother when they arrived home.

WHY OLD MR. OWL AWAKES AT NIGHT

One bright moonlight night, Scampy and Frisky were sound asleep. They woke up suddenly when they heard someone say in a loud voice "Who, who" - then it was quiet and then again the words were repeated. The little squirrels didn't know, what it was and were frightened.

They whispered together and Mother Squirrel heard them, "What's the matter?" she said very sleepily. "We heard a strange noise and didn't know what it was," they told her. "I heard it too" she told them, "that's just old Mr. Owl. He always makes more noise when the moon is bright."

The next morning they decided they'd try to find Mr. Owl and see why he made so much noise at night and kept others awake. They looked and looked but couldn't find him. Then suddenly they saw what they thought was a big bunch of feathers. There was Mr. Owl sound asleep with his head tucked under his wing.

They called and called him but he didn't hear; finally he pulled his head out from under his wing and blinked sleepily. "What do you want?" he said crossly, "Can't you see I'm asleep? Don't bother me!"

"Mr. Owl", said Scampy, "you're supposed to be very wise but I don't think you are. You sleep all day when the sun shines and there are so many beautiful things to see, and then when it's time to go to bed, you wake up."

Mr. Owl opened his eyes wide - nobody had ever talked to him like this before. "Well," he said rubbing his chin thoughtfully, "maybe you're right - I never thought about it that way."

"Yes," said Frisky, "we played hard all day yesterday and when we'd gone to bed tired, you made so much noise, we couldn't sleep."

"My, my" said old Mr. Owl, "I'm sorry - I always talk at night you know, but I wouldn't want to disturb you - my, my." "Maybe I better call a conference of all the owls in the woods and talk this matter over."

He was so bothered and upset, he couldn't go back to sleep, but put on his big spectacles, and sat very still, deep in thought. He didn't even notice when Scampy and Frisky scampered away.

"That was a good idea to talk to Mr. Owl," said Scampy. "I have an idea he won't wake us up at night any more."

52200851R00027

Made in the USA
Columbia, SC
01 March 2019